BRER
RABBIT
retold

ARTHUR FLOWERS JAGDISH CHITARA

Brer Rabbit retold

Copyright © 2017 Tara Books Pvt. Ltd.
For the text: Arthur Flowers
For the illustrations: Jagdish Chitara

For this edition:
Tara Books Pvt. Ltd., India
www.tarabooks.com
and
Tara Publishing Ltd., UK
www.tarabooks.com/uk

Design: Tanuja Ramani
Cover design: Catriona Maciver
Production: C. Arumugam

Printed and bound by AMM Screens, Chennai, India.

ISBN: 978-93-83145-46-1

BRER RABBIT
retold

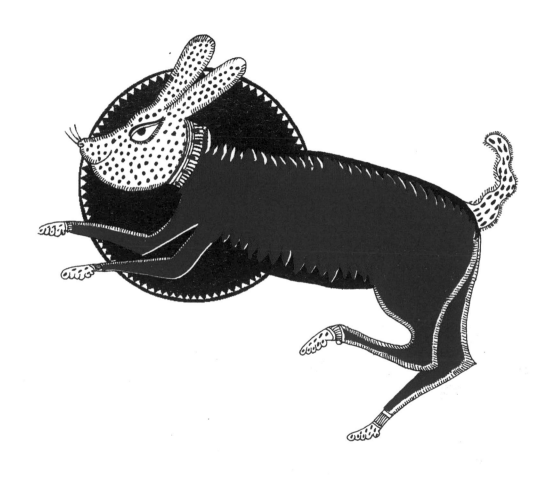

ARTHUR FLOWERS JAGDISH CHITARA

BRER RABBIT
and the big party

I am Flowers of the Delta Clan Flowers and the line of O Killens, I am mythmaker, devoted servant of the word and sometimes its master, these tales I tell as they were told to me. **Ibayo**.

The Brer Rabbit stories were originally told by a small cadre of slave storytellers on a middling plantation in Georgia. One of these slaves, one Uncle George, the first African-American storyteller (well, 1st one to make the historical cut) was called Uncle Remus by Joel Chandler Harris, an Atlanta-based journalist who wrote them down after the South lost the Civil War.

He did this in part to depict a slavery that had contented both master and slave. He also had a sincere appreciation for the Brer Rabbit Tales, and had he not written them down they likely would not have survived as iconic cultural artifacts. But to make his case for slavery as a good thing he twisted them up some and many of them little more than narrative minstrelsy.

As a bona fide delta confabulator, I have long wanted to reclaim them—one of the sturdy roots of African-American culture/literature, and a repository of African-American Wisdom tales. Harris took them for his purposes, I'm taking them back for mine.

So. Giving this Work to Baba George Remus, him and Brer Rabbit, keeper of the stories. And BabaJohn Killens, of course. The Great Griot Master of Brooklyn. Master of the Longgame and he who taught me to see.

Cast your vision, young hoodoo, as far as you can see, determine the challenges the tribe will face, prepare the tribal soul to meet them.

Now, me and the Rabbit, we old friends. Sometime, when I'm back home in Memphis, kicking back alongside the banks of the Big Muddy, Brer Rabbit and them will take a notion to come calling.

I will be there in my sitting room. Minding my own. But then sometime, feeling like company I will close my eyes and pretend that I am asleep. Generally the animalfolk shy of humanfolk, won't talk to each other if they think we around to listen, but soon as they think I'm asleep, the door ease open and ol Brer Rabbit peep in just so.

When he see me with my eyes closed like that, he motion the rest of them in and before you know it, they having a party. Rabbit get to chopping his bluesharp, Brer Bear be beat beating on that hollow log of his and Big Mama Coon playing guitar bigger than she whilst Sistah and Brother Fox cutting up the rug and Brer Alligator acting a fool on the stride piano. O yes, truly a good time being had by all.

Sometime I forget myself and I think to join in the festivities and I open my eyes, but the minute I open them they all disappear. Till I sit back and close them again and there they are. Having a good old time. My guests. My friends. My family. My kin. Singing and dancing and telling you remember when stories I'm a tell you.

In the name of the Conqueror
Let these Tales be Told
God's Blessings on Us All

BRER RABBIT
and the tar baby

L isten if you will. A moment of your time, perhaps, invested whilst I tell you how Brer Rabbit can be so tricky slicky sometime. How just cause he weak don't mean he not free.

One day, I'm told, it come to pass that Brer Rabbit was hopping down the trail when he spy upon a tar baby sitting directly in his path.

Now I don't have to tell you it was Brer Fox set up that tar baby. Just that morning he come up with the idea of taking a doll and smearing it with the stickliest tar he could find. Then he set that tar baby out on Brer Rabbit's daily path.

When Brer Rabbit come along and spy that tar baby by the side of the road, he stop and say *Good morning, sir.* So far so good, but he take offense when the tar baby don't reply.

Next thing you know, Brer Rabbit selling wolf tickets, huffing and puffing himself up till he end up throwing a punch at the tar baby and find his right paw stuck. He mad now. He throw another punch. And another and another and now all four paws stuck, sure as you please.

At this point, Brer Fox come out of hiding, singing his brand new victory song. *I got you now, Brer Rabbit, I believe I have outfoxed you this time, get it, out Foxed you, o yes, this is good.*

Well yes, Brer Fox, say Brer Rabbit, *Look like you outfox this time. Onliest thing I ask is that you don't throw me into that briar patch. Whatever you do, don't do that.*

Why not the briar patch? Brer Fox ask him, referring to a big field of briar wilderness that's standing by, all brambly bush and thick

with thorns. Brer Rabbit commence to howling. *Not the briar patch, Brer Fox, anything but that.*

Don't you worry none about the briar patch, Brer Rabbit, I'm having you for supper. Brer Fox lick his chops and Brer Rabbit allow he liable to make a right tasty stew. *Anything but that briar patch.*

You really fear that briar patch that much, Brer Rabbit?

More than anything, Brer Fox.

Well, here you go then, Brer Rabbit, the old Fox say and he throw Brer Rabbit off into the briar patch. Brer Rabbit fall screaming into the bramble. Then the screaming stop and all Brer Fox hear is the sound of somebody scrambling off in the bushes, laughing and rustling about. *Is that you laughing, Brer Rabbit?* ask the Fox.

That's me laughing, Brer Fox, say the Rabbit. *I was born in the briar patch, Brer Fox. All you did was set me free.*

Then he scamper away. Just as free as he can be. This is the key that opens all locks, a master of strategy.

That is all. This Tale is done
God's Blessings on Us All

BRER ALLIGATOR
meet up with trouble

S it down, my friend, make yourself comfortable whilst I tell you what Brer Rabbit got to say about Trouble. Now, everybody know Trouble. Sooner or later, **Trou*ble*** come to us ALL.

But back in the day Brer Alligator did not know Trouble well. Brer Alligator was a pretty creature back then. Had that smooth pretty skin, thought he was better than everybody else. One day Brer Rabbit pass him by and say, pleasantly enough, *Good morning, Brer Alligator.*

Brer Alligator act like he don't see Brer Rabbit. Stick his long nose in the air. Well, it is a well-known fact Brer Rabbit quick to take offense—ask the tar baby if you don't believe me.

So. Brer Rabbit decide he will get back at Brer Alligator. So the next day, Brer Rabbit come hopping by distracted, looking at his watch and mumbling, *I'm late, I'm late, I'm really, really late.*

Now, anybody with the sense God gave a pecan know not to ask no rabbit talking about he late, what he late for, unless you ready to go through the looking glass. But Brer Alligator known to be a curious man, he say, *Where to, Brer Rabbit?*

I'm going to meet Trouble, say Brer Rabbit, *Surely you know Trouble, he a big man in these parts, own all the land.*

Brer Alligator say, *Well no, don't believe I know him, sound like somebody I need to know, mind if I tag along?* Brer Rabbit say, *Sure, bring the family.*

Now that's just mean, down and dirty mean. Brer Rabbit take the whole Alligator family to that big field down by the riverside. That's when he tell the Alligator family, *Y'all wait right here, I'm going to get Trouble.*

Then he go over to the other side of the field and he start a great big fire, and soon enough that fire is snappling and crackling, with great red, yellow and orange leaping flames.

Now, riddle me this—very often you can see Trouble coming. You can see Trouble coming miles down the road. But sometime Trouble come wrapped up in that pretty packaging, those red, yellow and orange leaping flames, and instead of getting out of the way, you be talking about, *My, my, that looks good. I'ma get me some of that, I'ma get me some of that Trouble.*

So. Instead of moving out the way, the alligator family standing by, waiting on Trouble.

CHORUS: THEY WAITING ON TROUBLE

After awhile that fire come up on them and Sistah Alligator raise her long nose in the air. She say, *I think I smell Trouble.* But they don't move. Cause they waiting on Trouble. And after awhile that fire got them surrounded. And one of the little Alligator children say, *I think I feel Trouble. Deep down in my soul. And I believe we need to move.*

CHORUS: THEY NEED TO MOVE

And they. Right next to the water. But to. Get to the water. They have to. Go through the fire.

So the Alligator family, they scoot through the fire and into the water. And they get away. But they get all scorched up.

And that's why. To this day. When you see Brother Alligator. He will have a wrinkled up skin.

And that's why. To this day. When you see Sistah Alligator. She won't be too far from the water.

And that's why. To this day. When you speak to them little Alligators for more than a minute or two. They will tell you. Into each life. There must be **Trou***ble*. Battles nobody else could win. But don't. Go looking for **Trou***ble*. Not unless **Trou***ble*. Comes looking for you.

That is all. This Tale is done
hold on, ibayo, hold on

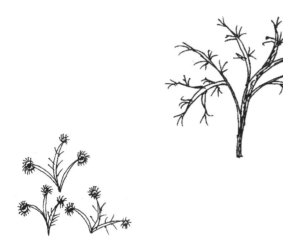

SISTAH RABBIT
and the big wind

Sometime tradition, you got to play with it a little, keep it fresh, ahead of the curve, poetic dispensation, shall we say. This next story about Brer Rabbit's sister. I say she just as slick as the Rabbit, somefolk say she slicker. Ask anybody around these parts and they will tell you about Sistah Rabbit and the big wind.

Wahoo

How, back in the day, when the world was still young, all the little animals lived together in peace and harmony, until the day come there was a huge, long drought, and there was no more food and drinking water. Except over in The Clayton Field.

In The Clayton Field, they got a tree heavy burdened with the most succulent fruits and vegetables, with peaches, mango, corn, watermelon and broccoli, everything grow on the Tree of Life, fully stocked in every season, with seeds that's good for growing things.

The Clayton Field also had a pool of pure, clean drinking water, enough for all the little animals in the forest, all their family and community needs. But The Clayton Field was claimed by Brer Tiger, and Brer Tiger was not inclined to share.

Consequently, all the creatures of the forest was hungry and thirsty, poor little things, one by one just fading away. Finally, Sistah Rabbit call a meeting to order. She declare it wasn't right for one creature to hold onto all the food and drinking water whilst the rest of us just fading away. She told them she had a plan. Upon hearing her plan they all agree. *By God, that's a mighty fine plan.*

So the next day, all the little creatures in God's green heaven take up their positions whilst Brer Tiger still sleep. When he finally arise, here come Sistah Rabbit with a big rope slung over her shoulder, singing a warning song so loud she wake the sun:

Lord, Lord, there's a big wind coming
Gonna blow everybody off the face of the earth, Let
me take a minute, Lord, let me tie them all down
so they don't blow away, Lord, don't blow away

Just then a sound like you never, never heard. Brother Bear start beating on a old hollow log.

Bigga bam bam, boogie boogie, bam bam, boom.

And the Buzzard and the Eagle start flapping their wings, and the wind is a blowing and the trees are a bending and the little bitty creatures just a running all around and they shaking up the bushes and they shaking up the ground and it sound like a big wind coming gonna blow everybody off the face of the earth. *Well, what you waiting for,* say Brer Tiger, *Tie me,* he say, *Tie me tight.*

Ain't got time to tie you, Brer Tiger, say Sistah Rabbit, *I got to tie all the little creatures down. They the ones gon blow off the face of the earth.*

Bigga bam bam, boogie boogie, bam bam, boom.

Tie me first, Sistah Rabbit, Brer Tiger told her with a snarling tonality. *Else I'm gon have to take a bite out of you, Sistah Rabbit, biggest bite ever been took.*

Well, Brer Tiger, since you put it like that. She commence to tying. She tie and she tie and she tie. Then she step back and admire her handiwork. *How about that, Brer Tiger, you tied up tight?*

Got a little movement in my shoulder, Sistah Rabbit. Best you tie me a little tighter.

So. Sistah Rabbit tie and she tie and she tie and she tie. *How about that now, Brer Tiger, I believe I got you tight.*

Brer Tiger try to wiggle. *I can't move Sistah Rabbit. You have tied me up tight.*

That's good, Brer Tiger, that's exactly the way we want you. Tied up tight.

Then Sistah Rabbit motion her paw and all the noise stop and all the little creatures come out, gathering round Brer Tiger, laughing and joking and signifying like folk sometime do when they got the upper hand on you.

Brer Tiger realize he been had. He roar and he roar, but he tied up tight.

Then all the little animals form a workline pulling apples, corn, watermelon and broccoli off the Tree of Life. And over at the stream they passing out buckets of pure, cool drinking water. And whilst they working, they singing one of them oldtimey worksongs:

This is the way. We work together.
Cause when we. Work together.
Ain't nothing. We can't do

That is all. This Tale is done
Ain't nothing we can't do

BRER RABBIT
and Sistah Turtle

Now there was once upon a time that the Rabbit was bested. Wouldn't want you to think he won all the time. Everybody have to lose sometime, that's what make life interesting.

I recall once or twice Sistah Turtle got the best of him. Back in the day, Sistah Turtle was a slow boat to Memphis. I suspect she still so, but one day she decide to teach the old Trickster a lesson.

I tell you what I'ma do, Brer Rabbit, she say one day out the clear blue, *you call yourself a fast runner. I bet I can beat you to that creek 3 miles down the road. I will put good money on that, Brer Rabbit.*

This sound like easy money to Brer Rabbit. The bet is on and Sistah Turtle position herself on the road leading to the creek. *When you hear me count three, you light out,* she say, *I will be right there with you.*

Now what happen is this. Sistah Turtle got two fullgrown children and each one look just like her. So Sistah Turtle, she put Eldest Son Turtle at the 2-mile post and got her Babygirl Turtle at the 1-mile post, both of them with their heads facing the creek. Then she position her old man, Brer Turtle, right at the creek with his head sitting in the water.

Then Sistah Turtle say, *One, two, three, go.*

Brer Rabbit light out. Get to the 2 mile marker and Eldest Son Turtle yell out, *I'm here, Brer Rabbit.*

Rabbit say, *How you get here so fast?*

Eldest Son Turtle say, *I'm running so fast you can't see me, Brer Rabbit.*

Rabbit say, *See this*, and he light out, running harder than he has ever run before, running so hard he leave his shadow in the dust. But when he get to the 1-mile marker, Babygirl Turtle yell, *I'm here, Brer Rabbit. Best you pick it up.*

Brer Rabbit pick it up. My God, does he pick it up. But when he get to the creek, Brer Turtle yell out, *Here I am, Brer Rabbit.* Then he duck down into the water.

You win, Sistah Turtle, say Brer Rabbit, *Ain't nobody fast as you. Usually, I'ma little quicker than I was today. I must have pulled a muscle or something.*

Brer Turtle raise his head out the creek and say, *I tell you what I will do, Brer Rabbit. I will give you another chance. I will turn around and race you back.*

Deal! say Brer Rabbit, and he light out quicker than quick.

At the 1-mile marker, Babygirl hear him coming and turn around so her head face the other way. Rabbit come panting up and Babygirl Turtle yell, *I'm here, Brer Rabbit.*

How can that be? Rabbit light out even harder now, running harder than anybody has ever run before, and he pretty wore out at the 2-mile marker, where Eldest Son Turtle waiting for him, turned about and talking trash, *What's taking you so long, Brer Rabbit?*

Rabbit don't even try to make the third marker. He just lie there and declare Sistah Turtle the fastest creature he has ever seen. *So, so,* Eldest Son Turtle say, *so, so.*

Now, when Brer Rabbit recount this tale, he will likely tell you that he took a nap or some such, and that's why Sistah Turtle beat him. To this day, it perplex him how he could get beat by a Turtle.

Now, Sistah Turtle, she tell anybody that listen how she like to run that Rabbit to death, 3 miles coming and going, and them

Turtles ain't moved, except to turn around and face the other way.

Brer Rabbit, it don't cross his mind, not for a minute, that somebody trick the trickster. Rabbit see a Turtle now, he run the other way. The humiliation more than he can stand.

That is all. This Trick is done.
God's Blessings on Us All

SISTAH GROUNDHOG
and the long look

O nce upon a time all tales were songs. This one bout the time Brer Rabbit and Brer Bear was sitting on a lowslung hill in the middle of the Delta, disputing on who the best. It was Brer Rabbit started it, when he claim, *For no reason that I can see, Ain't nobody in the world good as me.*

Weell nooow, drawl Brer Bear, with that ponderous dignity accompany everything he do, *That's exactly what folk say about me.*

But look at these ears, say Brer Rabbit, showing off his long fluffy ears. *Aint these bout the prettiest ears you ever seen? Nobody in the world can hear like me. Watch and learn, Brer Bear, or should I say Listen.*

With that, his ears stand up on his head like radar antenna quartering the sky, till finally he say, *Do you see that mountain yonder there, Brer Bear? On the side of that mountain I hear a bee buzzing a honey tree, and I can tell from the nature of the buzz that the honey is sweet. What do you think about that, Brer Bear?*

Weell nooow, say Brer Bear, *I acknowledge that accomplishment, Brer Rabbit. But I do have to wonder, how well can you smell?*

Whereupon Brer Bear commence to sniffing the air, nose quivering, snorting, and swivelating for the rest of the day, till finally he say, *OK then, Brer Rabbit, I have smelled far enough. Did you notice that in that honey tree there is a nest, and in that nest there are two eggs. I smelled that the far hand egg is a wee bit stale.*

So now they arguing over which is better, smell or hearing. This disputation go on all night and into the next day, when they hear a little tiny sound from the ground and look down to see Little Sistah Groundhog po^king her head out of her abode.

Hey fellas, say Little Sistah Groundhog, *I'm trying to get some Workings done down here but I can't think for all this noise. It's been made clear by now, to one and all, that you can smell and hear better than most, but I wonder how far can you see.*

Rabbit and Bear look at each other and peruse the horizon, trying to see who see the best. But before either can speak, Little Sistah Groundhog come out and settle herself. *Now you two sit right there,* she say, *and I'ma run a little test to determine who the best on this hill.*

Then Little Sistah Groundhog refocus most strange, staring into the horizon with a mighty gaze, that went on for days and days and days, till finally Brer Bear clear his throat and ask *Weeell, Little Sistah, how far did you look and what did you see?*

Little Sistah Groundhog say, *Fellas, when I took that look, it was the longest look that's ever been took. I looked all over the world and beyond, even took me a quick peak out amongst the stars and all the universes, o I seen everything there is to see, all the way back to this very hill, and what do I see on this hill but two of the biggest fools the world has ever seen. Who got nothing better in the world to do than argue about who better than who.*

Muttering with disgust, she return to her abode, but they can still hear her tiny little voice grumbling down below:

That's all, she say, this Tale is done. God's Blessings on saints and fools alike, ibayo

BRER WOLF
got a plan

S o. Let me tell you about the time, pretty much all the time, Brer Wolf and Brer Fox was pondering ways to corner Brer Rabbit. *What we got to do*, say Brer Wolf, *is we got to trap him.*

I have tried many times to trap that Rabbit, say Brer Fox. *How you plan to go about it?*

We will get him to come to your house of his own free will, say the Wolf, *then we trap him.*

Have him jump in the pot of his own free will? say the Fox. *That's some powerful trickerating.*

Trust me in this matter, say the Wolf. *I'ma do the fooling, you do the catching. What I need you to do now is go home and play dead, and when he come by to offer his condolences I will come up behind him, and between us, we snatch him right up. Rabbit stew for everybody.*

Brer Fox agree it sound like plan to him, so he take to his bed and he lie there all stiffed up like he has pulled up dead. Meanwhile, Brer Wolf go to Brer Rabbit's house and knock on the door. *Who there?* ask the Rabbit.

A friend, say the Wolf.

Well, say the Rabbit, *there this kind of friend and there that kind of friend. Which kind of friend are you?*

A friend that's fetching bad news, say the Wolf.

That kind of friend, say the Rabbit, *state your business. Friend.*

Have you heard, the Wolf tell him, *ol Brer Fox has died in his sleep. Somebody need to go sit with the body whilst I fetch my mourning gown.*

Brer Wolf trot off and Brer Rabbit think about it. The demise of Brer Fox would certainly make his life easier, but good news hard to trust less it's been verified.

Brer Rabbit decide to drop round Brer Fox's house to see how the land lay. When he get to Brer Fox's house, the door is open. He find that peculiar for a security-minded fellow like Brer Fox. So he stop at the door, kinda alert, and first thing he spy is Brer Fox stretched out on the bed, deader than dead.

Brer Rabbit look around and he ponder the significations. Then he mutter aloud, *Shame nobody around to look after Brer Fox. Not even Brer Turkey Buzzard come to arrange the funeral. It's the busy season for me but I will set up with him if there nobody else to do it. Onliest thing is I don't know if Brer Fox really dead, cause generally folk that's seriously dead will every once in awhile raise their hind leg up and holler Wahoo!*

Brer Fox don't twitch, Brer Fox don't move. He has not heard of these particular funeral proceedings, and he don't quite trust the rabbit.

Guess I will be moving on, say Brer Rabbit, *No sense in hanging around here, cause if Brer Fox was really dead, by now he would have raised up his hind leg and yelled Wahoo for sure.*

At that point, Brer Fox raise up his hind leg and yell, *Wahoo!*

Wahoo yourself, say Brer Rabbit, and he light out, resolving never ever to return to Brer Fox's door never ever no more.

From now on, he say, *I'ma tend to the living, let the dead take care of the dead.*

**That is all, this Tale is done –
God's Blessings on Us All**

Wahoo!

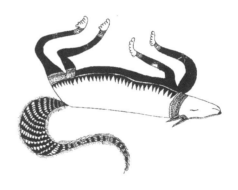

BRER RABBIT
& the goober patch

Once upon a time, back when all tales were true, and all lies too, Brer Fox had this pretty good goober patch. By and by, it become clear somebody stealing his goobers.

So. One day he set a trap for the thief, and before you know it, here come Brer Rabbit caught up in Brer Fox's trap net, dangling from a tree in the middle of Brer Fox's peanut field.

Presently, Brer Bear come lumbering down the road and Brer Rabbit hail him, *Howdy Brer Bear,* say the Rabbit. Brer Bear look around to see who howdying him this early in the morning. When he see Brer Rabbit hanging there, he wonder what's what.

Why helloo there, Brer Rabbit, say Brer Bear all slooow and deliberate like he tend to be. *How you coming along this morning?* he say.

Fair to middling, say the Rabbit.

Well noow, any particular reason you up there consorting with the elements? say Brer Bear. *Strike me a tad uncomfortable.*

Making a dollar a minute scarecrowing for Brer Fox, say the Rabbit, *I wouldn't mind taking a break, but at a dollar a minute I can't afford too much of a break.*

A dollar a minute? inquire Brer Bear. *A dollar a minute.* say Brer Rabbit. *How long you need that break?* ask Brer Bear. *Ten, fifteen minutes,* say Brer Rabbit. *Ten, fifteen minutes?* ask Brer Bear. *Ten, fifteen minutes,* say Brer Rabbit.

Welll Brer Rabbit, say Brer Bear, *for a dollar a minute I will scarecrow for you whilst you take your break.*

So. Brer Rabbit and Brer Bear exchange places. When Brer Fox come by to see who been caught up in his trap, it's Brer Bear he find hanging there.

So you the one been stealing my goobers. For shame, Brer Bear, for shame. Whereupon Brer Fox pick up a stick and get to whupping Brer Bear so bad he can't get a word in edgewise.

When Brer Bear finally do get loose from there, first thing he do is go to find Brer Rabbit. When he catch up with the Rabbit, he is in a very bad mood. Snarling, slobbering, and such. A bad bear state of mind. He about to do the Rabbit harm when Brer Rabbit ask him did he get paid.

Paid? say Brer Bear. *Paid,* say the Rabbit. *How long were you up there?*

Ten, Fifteen minutes, Brer Bear say. *Ten, Fifteen minutes?* say Brer Rabbit. *Ten, fifteen minutes,* say Brer Bear, repeating it again and again, as he lumber off looking for Brer Fox and his lost wages.

When Brer Bear don't get paid he will most likely blame the Rabbit. Some folk never learn. Never, never, NEVER learn. Some folk don't even recognize the question. Best you be one who do. Best you be one that see. Spiritvision, my kind call it. Always more interesting what's going on beneath the surface of things.

That is all, this tale is done. God's Blessings on them that see

QUEEN MOTHER MAMMY BAMMY & the lucky mojo

In the old days, when time was still a callow youth, it was considered good luck to carry a Rabbit's foot. Back in the day Brer Rabbit had five. It was Queen Mother Mammy Bammy Big Money, the local witchbunny, gave him that extra foot. Back when he was a young rabbit and prone to taking unnecessary chances.

These days you do best to get you a John the Conquer root and be done with it, but in the old days, before cities replace the grassland, it was a rabbit's foot considered the most powerful mojo on earth.

Now Brer Rabbit, as is his wont, had been keeping the neighborhood unsettled with his relentless trickeration. His neighbors have pondered long and hard how to restrain him, but all the plans, traps, tricks, and jugglements in the world come to naught when it come to the Rabbit. He outtrick them all.

Sistah Turtle, recently nominated to a Judgeship, say she think the Rabbit is a conjure. *A trickster for sure,* say Brer Bear. *Or in cahoots with one,* say Brer Fox, *that Rabbit got more luck than smarts.*

Well, say Big Mama Coon, *the real question is why all the luck on his side? That's what I want to know.* That's when Judge Turtle note that Brer Rabbit always got his lucky foot with him. *That's likely where he keep his mojo,* say she.

The rest of the animals agree. And so. Brer Fox is assigned to get the Rabbit's mojo. First chance he get he snatch Brer Rabbit's extra foot through an open window. When Brer Rabbit notice his lucky foot gone, he look high and low before deciding he has lost it. His first thought is that his mojo been so good, surely he can coast on it for awhile.

But when you lose your mojo, it's just not the same. Throws your cosmic game off. Next thing you know, Brer Fox got all the luck, Brer Rabbit ain't got a lick. Brer Fox getting rich, Brer Rabbit can't keep a dime on a dime. After he been almost captured twice, he go see Queen Mother Mammy Bammy Big Money, quick quick.

Yes, I know. Lotta name for a little rabbit, but in the old days, a witchrabbit get to name herself and that was her entitlement. The Queen Mother part she earned. Now, as most everybody know, including you one would hope, Queen Mother Mammy Bammy live off in the Dismal Swamp somewhere, and to get to her you had to:

ride some, slide some, jump some, hump some
hop some, flop some, walk some, balk some
creep some, sleep some, fly some, cry some
foller some, holler some, suukie suukie suukie some

And then even then, unless you most monstrously careful, you just might miss her. Fortunately, Brer Rabbit know the way. Carefully he make his way to the crossroads, where the highroad cross the low, and there he see this black smoke that rise up out the ground and become mist.

Mammy Bammy do like her drama. She believe in getting your attention. Vaguely, he see her off in there somewhere but if you look too hard she will disappear, so he address the mist like he suppose to. *Queen Mother, Mammy Bammy, I need your help.*

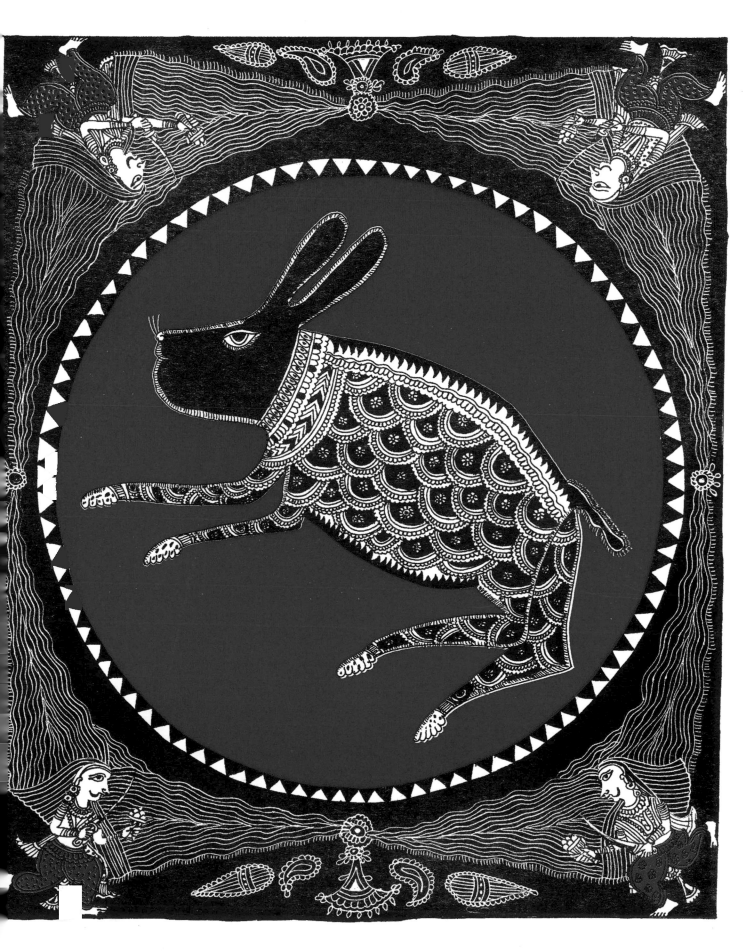

And what help would that be, Son Rabbit? Mammy Bammy ask him, words all breezy like they just more mist. *What can your need possibly be?*

It go without saying that Mammy Bammy know his need. Mammy Bammy know everything worth knowing. Know you when you walk in her door better than you know yourself. She just playing with him, now.

I lost the extra foot you gave me, Queen Mother, all my mojo gone with it.

You ain't lost it, she say. *Brer Fox stole your luck is what happened. Carrying your luck in his left front pocket. Got a gold chain clipping it to his belt.*

Then the Queen Mother suck that mist back into wherever it go and she **disappear** with it. So. OK. Brer Rabbit set out for home, muttering about the injustice of it all. Then he get busy. Watching Brer Fox like Sistah Hawk do it. Ain't got time to notice his luck gone bad.

Then one day he note Brer Fox leave home without his lucky foot. Fore long here come Brer Rabbit, knocking on the door. Sistah Fox open up and say, *How do, Brer Rabbit, how you making it this morning?*

Fair to middling, Sistah Fox. Brer Rabbit remove his hat and put on his smile. *Excuse my intrusion, Sistah, but Brer Fox left his lucky foot, and he ask me to come fetch it for him.*

Now Sistah Fox know well as anybody that the Rabbit is not to be trusted, but also she know that rabbit foot don't belong to her man, and good-hearted creature that she is—head usher over at the Downhome Baptist Church, first one to catch you when the spirit come calling—she hand it over and wish him well.

So Brer Rabbit got his foot back. But his fabled mojo don't return with it. Old boy's luck about the same as everybody else

—hit and miss. By and by, he go back to Mammy Bammy and he ask her where his mojo gone.

You still got your share, the Queen Mother tell him, same as everybody else. *Still got 4 feet right, count yourself ahead of the game.*

But I'm not as fast as I used to be, Mammy Bammy. I'm not as sharp as I used to be. I lost my luck and my mojo, too.

Getting old, Son Rabbit, ain't got nothing to do with luck. That's just maturity calling, play it right and you benefit.

Brer Rabbit is not convinced. Want his mojo back like it always been. *I need your Blessing Mammy Bammy, I need it bad.*

Queen Mother Mammy Bammy Big Money give the matter due consideration. Then she point out Brer Rattlesnake lounging in the sun. *I want you to catch me that rattler there, Brer Rabbit, I want you to do that for me.*

Now when Queen Mother Mammy Bammy Big Money task you to do something, you don't ask her why, you just comply. Brer Rabbit ponder the matter for a moment or two, then he tie up a noose in a rope and he approach Brer Snake.

Morning, Brer Snake, say Brer Rabbit. *Sorry to disturb your rest, but me and Mammy Bammy here trying to decide just how long you are. She say you about 3 feet long, I say no, Brer Snake is at least 4. Do you mind stretching out full length so I can measure you with this here rope?*

Not at all, Brer Rabbit, say Brer Snake. *I believe I am at least 5, myself.*

So Brer Snake proudly stretch himself out and, quick quick, Brer Rabbit got him roped, long angry body whipping about and shaking his long tail rattle.

My sincerest apologies, Brer Snake, Brer Rabbit say, *This Mammy Bammy's doing, not mine.*

He hope that suffice, cause Brer Snake is not someone you want as a mortal enemy. First thing Mammy Bammy do is release Brer

Snake and ease his irritation with the promise of lifetime free consultation. *Everytime you shed your skin,* she say, *everytime you start anew.*

After Brer Snake wiggle off a satisfied customer, she say *Well, Son Rabbit, that took you all of 5 minutes. If you was any sharper than that the rest of God's creatures would be in danger.*

The Queen Mother suck her smoke back into the earth and all he hear then is like her echo.

Awaken the sleeper, protect the weak, guide the strong
That's Blessing enuf for anybody. ibayo ibayo ibayo

BRER RABBIT
& the people who could fly

This tale, Old Man Rabbit told me straight up. I suspect he took liberties with the truth, and for this tale I will not vouch. You be the judge on this one, I will not testify.

According to the Rabbit, he was amongst the first batch of captives brought over from the old country. Old Man Rabbit told me the slaves was understandably unhappy with their new condition. Say he did not himself appreciate working like a slave and took to crawling into the bush till the evening bell ring. That's how he come to miss the departure.

This is a story, a story he has told me many times, same chair, same story, so many times I could tell it myself, but each time he tell me something new. It was, the Old Rabbit said most thoughtfully, last time he told me this, an uncommonly hot day they left him behind. They had been working the fields when the overseer attempt to whip a young woman what was carrying a little babychild on her back, little did he know that the Conqueror was in the field that day.

It was Zora Neale, Old Man Rabbit told me, that claim the Conqueror was a slaverytime hoodoo that trick old master out of freedom. Say when Freedom come, the spirit of the Conqueroo withdraw into the Conqueror Root, to return whenever the folk in need. It was Zora Neale claim the Conqueror must ride on the wind cause he so fast. Claim he can be tending to a slave deep

in the Sudan when the whip sing in Mississippi and before the lash land on the back the Conqueror is in the house, and lo and behold, the woman with the babychild had **rose up** into the sky.

CHORUS: LO AND BEHOLD

That's what Zora Neale claim. Ask her yourself if you don't believe me. Or ask the Rabbit. I told you, I will not testify. The overseer was also amazed, he don't want to believe his lying eyes, either. Never seen anything like it in all his born days. But the slaves, they was not so much amazed. They been waiting for this moment, this very day.

CHORUS: FA AT THE CROSSROADS, TIME TO GO.

The Overseer try to get his discipline on but one by one they rise up and fly away back to Geeche Land. All this commotion wake up the Rabbit. Perceiving the moment, he try to join them, but by then they far, far, away, the faint mythwork of dust in the distance.

Not fair, he say. *Why I got to stay behind. With them,* he protest, indicating the earthbound slaves who had also been left, once again bending to their onerous tasks and singing a brand new blues. Hold on.

I need you here, Brer Rabbit, the Conqueror say. *Help me take care of the ones who no longer fly, the lucklost Children of the Sun, newly forged for journeys to come.*

The Conqueroo look up into the sky and count the stars in their many billions, *Stardust,* he say, *every molecule in your body, the detritus of stars that exploded long ago. That's all we are, Young Rabbit, stardust. Us and everything in the Universe. Got to get off the planet, you see, spread out and increase the odds. That's where you come in, Brer Rabbit, that's when you win your wings.*

**I myself I cannot fly. I will not testify
but all things are possible, ibayo**

BRER RABBIT
roll the rock

O nce upon a time, right on the edge of day and night and what look to be a full moon rising, Brer Rabbit walking along when he hear a mournful howl. **Whoop whoop whooooooo!**

Who there? ask the Rabbit when he hear that howl again, dancing on the edge of the rising moon. **Whoop whoop whooooooo!**

Then he hear an equally mournful voice, about as sad as it can be, asking if somebody would *please, please, come help a poor soul like me.*

The Rabbit is curious but he cautious, too. Rule is you don't want to answer when nobody call because it just might be a haint. But since when did Brer Rabbit follow rules. *Where are you,* he ask. *Who are you? Even better,* he ask, *what are you?*

I'm down in the gully here, he hear the haint say, *Brer Rabbit, is that you? This Brer Wolf. I fell off the road and there is a big rock on me.*

When Brer Rabbit caution over to the gully, he find Brer Wolf under a rock, howling so pitiful even Brer Rabbit feel sorry for him. He inclined to help a brother out but he hesitate. *I find it difficult to trust you, Brer Wolf, based on your past behavior.*

You can trust me in this, Brer Rabbit. Help me this one time and I will be your friend, forever and ever more.

Now Brer Rabbit generally an astute practitioner of urban survival skills, specially when it come to the local predatorial community. But he decide the gamble is worth the price of the ticket. Friendship with the powerful is nothing to be sneered at.

So Brer Rabbit hoist his coattail up and he slide down to help Brer Wolf. He put his back to the rock and the pedal to the metal and he roll the rock right off. But the minute he free, Brer Wolf grab him up by the collar.

Brer Rabbit kick and he squeal, but Brer Wolf got him yoked up tight. Then Brer Rabbit ask if this is the way he thank folk that help him out like that.

O I will thank you, say the Wolf, *I'ma thank you for this meal I am about to receive. Don't hold this against me, Brer Rabbit, my family got to be fed same as yours. You do understand, you a family man, a wolf got to do what wolf got to do.*

I will never again do you a favor, say the Rabbit.

You will never again do anybody a favor, say the Wolf.

Where I come from, say Brer Rabbit, *it's against the law to kill folks that's done you a good turn. I suspect that's the law everywhere.*

Now Brer Wolf been applying for a position with the Humanfolk. Ever since Cousin Dog took up with the Humans, he been fat and happy, stretched out by the fire every evening, eating regular, kicking back in his dedicated rocking chair. Brer Wolf do not want to break the law if he can help it. Old boy been feral long enough.

They get to disputing what the law say about harming folk that's done you a good turn when Judge Turtle happen to walk by in all her ponderous dignity. They take advantage of this fortuitous opportunity and put their cases before her. Brer Wolf tell his side, Brer Rabbit tell his.

Judge Turtle put her specs on and she look at the issue from all sides. She take her time, as she is liable to do, and deliberate for some hours before she clear her throat and say, *This is a confusing dispute. I am. Uncertain.*

Perhaps, say the Rabbit, *it would help in your deliberations if you was to see the original situation.*

And what would that be? ask the Judge. Brer Rabbit's suggestion is this. That we roll this rock back over Brer Wolf. *Then you will watch while I roll it off. I'm sure you will judge it to be an act of uncommon mercy.*

Judge Turtle allow that sound like a case study to her. Brer Wolf is not overly enthusiastic about the idea, but he hungry for some rabbit stew and he rather not have to break the law to get it. So the Judge ask him to get back under the rock. *Just to see how the procedure went,* she say. *Won't take but a minute. I see already this case is liable to be adjudicated in your favor.*

So. Brer Wolf get back under the rock and he allow them to roll it back on him. Then Brer Rabbit and Judge Turtle stand there discussing the particulars of the case—the weight of the rock, shape and size, how it lie, what it will take to rock it, what it will take to roll it.

Excuse me, say Brer Wolf, *Could y'all hurry along with the deliberations? This rock is heavier than it was before.*

But Brer Rabbit and Judge Turtle continue to debate the evidence at hand. *Was it just like that?* ask the Judge. *Just like that,* say Brer Rabbit. Then they talk about the weather and the rumor Judge Turtle will be running for office soon. By and by, Judge Turtle remove her spectacles and say, *You was wrong, Brer Rabbit, to interfere with Brer Wolf in his daily doings. He was tending to his business, you need to tend to yourn. I find you guilty, Brer Rabbit, of abysmal foolishness.*

Brer Wolf commence to howling about an appeal, but Judge Turtle amble on off. **Whoop whoop whoo**₀₀**ooo**⁰⁰. Then Brer Wolf ask Brer Rabbit to help him out again, *This one last time, Brer Rabbit, I have learnt my lesson,*

This vow is touching in its sincerity, it is a new Wolf, steeped in redemption, that lies under that rock. But Brer Rabbit shake his

head, no. *Sorry, Brer Wolf, I don't believe so. Fool me once, shame on you. Fool me twice, shame on me.*

Brer Wolf commence to howling again, but Brer Rabbit don't hear it this time. **Whoop whoop whooooooo. whoop whoop whoooooo** , indeed.

You might, can though, when the moon rise just so. I suspect Brer Wolf still under that rock, calling out to everybody that pass: *please please, please, help a poor soul like me.*

Whoop whoop whoooooooo
ibayo ibayo ibayo

41

BRER RAM
defend himself

Back when time was just a notion, before Brer Wolf got stuck under that rock, he had been picking off Brer Ram's little lamb children whenever he could. Whenever they would stray too far from home, here come Brer Wolf with his teeth showing.

He didn't mess with Brer Ram though. Respectful of his sharp horns and his resentful nature, Brer Wolf left Brer Ram alone. But the day come, that him and Brer Fox happen upon each other and agree they so hungry that a little lamb just won't do. Don't make no sense to be this hungry when Brer Ram just rolling in fat.

But he scare me, allow Brer Fox, *what with those sharp horns and those red eyes of his. I believe he is a conjureman.*

Brer Wolf laugh at Brer Fox's trepidation and wonder aloud what kind of predator is it that's scared of sheep, even one with horns.

Well, say Brer Fox, *I hear you talking, Brer Wolf, but I have not noticed that you in too big a hurry to make a meal of him, either. I tell you what, Brer Wolf, I'm willing to go after him if you will keep me company.*

Just then a little puff of wind come up on them and Brer Fox jump like somebody up on him. Brer Wolf laugh out loud, *I don't think you the man I want beside me. When it get hot, I expect you to run off and leave me to do all the fighting.*

Brer Fox declare that ain't so. *You wound me to the quick, Brer Wolf, I'm as much predator as you are. Bit more subtle perhaps, but just as fierce.*

That's when Brer Fox suggest they tie themselves together so that neither one can leave the other. *I'ma tie my tail to your tail, and yours to mine. Then we both go get him.*

Brer Wolf allow that sound like a plan. So they tie their tails together and they go to Brer Ram's house. Brer Fox lagging a little, but Brer Wolf has shamed him and he good to go.

When they get to Brer Ram's house, he sitting there on the front porch, fiddling his fiddle. When he see them come over the hill tied together like that, he put the fiddle down and he holler out, *I'm much obliged to you, Brer Fox, for leading him here like you said you would. My smoke house running short, but everything be fine once we salt ourselves some wolfmeat. I'ma pickle you up some just like we agreed. Fetch him here, Brer Fox, fetch him here.*

Then Brer Ram get to pawing the ground and breathing red smoke. *Fetch him here, Brer Fox, fetch him here.*

Thats when Brer Wolf break and run, dragging Brer Fox behind him, tail to tail and tail to tail. Took them some time to untangle those tails. In fact, they might still be tangled. And to this day, they might go for a lamb now and then, but they don't mess with one that's got horns. That paw the ground and blow red smoke.

Prey and predator, predator and prey
God's Blessings on them both, ibayo

BRER TURTLE
try to fly

Once upon a time, when the world was much bigger than it is now, Brer Turtle take it in his head that he want to fly. One day, Brer Buzzard light on a limb to check out some likely prospects when Brer Turtle come sliding out the river and waddle up behind him.

Howdy, Brer Buzzard, he say. Brer Buzzard so startled he near fall of his limb. *Lord have mercy, Brer Turtle, you really gave me a fright. How you doing this morning?* says he.

Feeling poorly, Brer Buzzard, say Brer Turtle. *A pain here, a catch yonder, the cramps thrown in where they please, but I ain't complaining, nothing more than what a body my age can expect, specially one that has spent his whole life crawling on his belly. I thank the Lord I'm still able.*

Brer Buzzard begin to commiserate, but Brer Turtle interrupt him. *I'd be mighty appreciative,* he say, *if you taught me how to fly, Brer Buzzard.*

Why you want to do that? ask Brer Buzzard.

Seem to me that flying is a most wonderful thing, say Brer Turtle. *Been crawling on my belly since I can remember. I can't imagine anything better than to fly free of this hard packed earth.*

But nobody I know can swim like you swim, Brer Turtle. Nobody I know can walk and swim, too.

I want it all, Brer Buzzard, I want to walk, I want to swim, I want to fly.

I don't know, Brer Turtle, say the Buzzard. *This flying is a very complicated business. Harder than it look.*

But Brer Turtle pay Brer Buzzard no mind, worry him half to death till Brer Buzzard give in. *I will take you up this one time. For old times sake. You sure this alright with the Judge. Last time I was in court, she done right by me.*

Brer Turtle is offended, claim he his own man, say he don't need permission to better himself. And so it come to be that Brer Buzzard squat down and allow Brer Turtle to climb up on his back. Turtle get a good grip and he settle in. *You can get started now,* say Brer Turtle. *Best be careful not to go over any rocks and ruts. Get to jolting me around and I'ma goner.*

Brer Buzzard start off flying easy, moving so slick and smooth that Brer Turtle allow not that much to this flying after all. *Didn't take me long to get the hang of this,* he say. *Shame on you, Brer Buzzard, for trying to keep this flying to yourself. I'ma slide on off and try it on my own, say Brer Turtle.*

I wouldn't do that, not today, too many pockets of bad air, today, say Brer Buzzard. *Let me take you on down, we will revisit your options tomorrow.*

But Brer Turtle real hardshell when he put his mind to something and before you know it, he slid right on off. Immediately, of course, he begin to fall, flapping his legs and wagging his tail to no avail, flipping over, over and over, till BLAM, he hit the ground flat out on his back. Wasn't for the hardness of his shell, he would have cracked wide open. As it is, he lie there dazed, assessing the damage and trying to catch his breath.

Brer Buzzard land beside Brer Turtle and inquire of his health. *How you feel, Brer Turtle?*

Truth be told, Brer Turtle say, *I feel a little ruint.*

I told you, Brer Turtle, that flying more than a notion.

I believe you are at fault here, Brer Turtle say as he try to flip himself rightside up. *I flew just fine. It was the landing lessons that was remiss.*

Brer Turtle shake one flipper, then the next. He stretch his neck and he wag his tail. Then he slide on into the river and Mama Big Muddy welcome him home. When he swim off, he so graceful look like he flying after all.

Sing your song the best you can, that way you can appreciate other folk singing theres, ibayo

BRER BUZZARD
learn to fly right

I recall when Ol Boy Buzzard once got on the wrong side of the Rabbit. One day not that long ago, Brer Rabbit and Brer Fox got to disputing who can leap furthest into the elements. They decide to meet the next day, to settle the matter once and for all.

Then Brer Fox find out Brer Rabbit has contracted with Brer Buzzard to catch hold of him when he leap and fly him further than anybody earthbound could. Brer Fox find Brer Buzzard and offer him a better deal. Say he will give Brer Buzzard a pot of gold to take Brer Rabbit up and drop him from a reasonable height. Rabbit stew for everybody. *What you think, Brer Buzzard, sound good?*

Buzzard say it sound good. Now generally Brer Buzzard don't care to kill his own food, but he figure a pot of gold season it up just right. *I'm the very man for this kind of business, Brer Fox. Have that pot of gold ready, because that rabbit good as dead.*

So. When time came for the trial, Brers Rabbit, Fox, and Buzzard was on hand, along with all the other creatures in the forest.

They flip a coin to see who will make the first leap and Brer Fox win the toss. He take a running start and he leap over a tree branch. Brer Rabbit say he is impressed. Then he jump on Brer Buzzard's back and the Buzzard rise up and sail off with him.

Now, Brer Rabbit expect Brer Buzzard to take him aways and set him down, just enough to win the bet. But Buzzard climb high into the elements and Brer Rabbit feel worriation come down on him. *You can take me back down now, Brer Buzzard.*

Instead Brer Buzzard laugh at him, *Me and Brer Fox got a deal, Brer Rabbit, and it don't include you. We got a big meal planned, and you the honored guest. I get the leftovers.*

Then Brer Buzzard get to flying like a dodo bird, flipping and dipping and sidestepping like he been possessed. Brer Rabbit holding for dear life when he suddenly grip Brer Buzzard around his neck tuff and squeeze with all his might. Brer Buzzard squawk and lose altitude. *Let me go, Brer Rabbit,* he squawk, but Brer Rabbit just squeeze him tighter. *Straighten up and fly right,* Brer Rabbit sing, *before I lose my cool.*

Let me breathe, Brer Rabbit, cry Brer Buzzard, steady losing altitude and blacking out whilst Brer Rabbit grip him tighter. *Straighten up and fly right,* the Rabbit sing, *before I lose my cool.*

With his last breath, Brer Buzzard commence to flying right and Brer Rabbit let him breathe. Brer Buzzard feel like he has just got a reprieve, a return ticket from the land of the dead. And as folk close to death will sometimes do, he offer to cut a deal with the Lord. *Let me get this Rabbit off my back, Lord, and you can depend on me, to be the best Buzzard a Buzzard can be.*

After flying Brer Buzzard all over the county, Brer Rabbit finally fly him back to where they started and collect his winnings.

Since then, Brer Buzzard don't try to make a meal of nothing still got a grip. He wait till they good and dead. And anytime you see him now, he in Undertaker Black, carrying himself with an unassailable dignity, representing best he know how, our ongoing quest to be greater than we are.

Straighten up and fly right
ibayo ibayo ibayo

BRER RABBIT
& the gold

Time was everytime Brer Rabbit see Brer Hawk he talking trash, loudly proclaiming Brer Hawk best stay up there where he belong, else he gon meet up with the thunder of the rabbit. Fist #1 and Fist #2. But when Brer Hawk drop down to discuss the matter, Brer Rabbit scamper off into the briar patch.

But then there come the day Brer Hawk on the wing when he spy Brer Rabbit unawares. Before you know it, he swoop down and has caught Brer Rabbit up in his talons. Brer Rabbit talk mighty greasy then. *I was just playing with you, Brer Hawk. Can't you take a joke? A raptor of your stature ain't got time for petty matters like this.*

But Brer Hawk got his neck feathers ruffled. *You been having your way round here long enough, Brer Rabbit, bout time somebody put paid to you, and I guess that somebody is me.*

What about my gold? say Brer Rabbit. *What I'm supposed to do with my gold?*

What gold? say Brer Hawk.

That pot of gold I got buried out there in The Clayton Field, say the Rabbit. *Who will take care of my gold?*

Don't you worry about the gold, say Brer Hawk, *point it out to me and I will take care of it.*

Right over there, the big tree in the middle of The Clayton Field, I got a pot of gold buried right there in the roots. You go dig it up and I will wait here for you.

But Brer Hawk don't trust Brer Rabbit and he tie him to the fence while he mosey over to the big tree and begin digging up the roots, pecking the ground with his beak like a chicken.

By and by, here come Brer Wolf. When he see Brer Rabbit already tied he can't believe his luck. He had sworn off Rabbit but this was more than a body can stand. *Well, well*, he say, *Rabbit stew for the wolf, today.*

Be with you in a minute, Brer Wolf, Brer Rabbit tell him, *soon as Brer Rooster find the gold.*

What gold? say the Wolf. *The gold I hid*, the Rabbit say, *soon as Brer Rooster find it I will fulfill my obligation with you.*

How much gold? say the Wolf. *A pot of gold*, say the Rabbit. *Where is this gold?* say the Wolf. *Have to show you*, say the Rabbit. *Untie me and I will take you there.*

The Wolf untie the Rabbit and Brer Rabbit lead Brer Wolf over to the Tree of Life. *Got to warn you, Brer Wolf*, the Rabbit say, *Brer Rooster might object to your claim.*

I can handle Brer Rooster, say the Wolf. They get to the Tree. It is obscured in a cloud of dust from Brer Hawk's vigorous pecking. Before Brer Rabbit can say a word, Brer Wolf howl, *What you doing with my gold, Brer Rooster?*

Then the Wolf leap in. Now, Brer Rooster known to be a scrapper, but Brer Hawk a raptor of another feather, all beak, claws and attitude. By the time Brer Wolf get himself loose, he all chewed up and apologizing profusely to Brer Hawk, who has taken to wing, circling high above the proceedings, and squawking complaints about being robbed of his gold.

Brer Wolf rise up from where he lie, and say, *Give me a hand, Brer Rabbit, Brer Rooster was in uncommonly good form, today. He like to laid me low.*

Brer Rabbit decline. *Feeling a little off myself, Brer Wolf, I'ma go get you some help.*

But I got the gold, Brer Rabbit, a whole pot of it, come on over here and get you some.

I wouldn't feel right taking your gold, Brer Wolf. Just leave me what
you don't need.

Come closer, Brer Rabbit, say the Wolf, *so I don't have to yell.*

That's why my ears so long, say the Rabbit, *I can hear quite well.*

Ok, then. No more Mr. Nicewolf. Brer Wolf try to leap up on it but he still limping from Brer Hawk's attentions, and Brer Rabbit scamper away.

And so it is, to this day, that Brer Rabbit still talking trash, Brer Wolf still howling his frustrations, and Brew Hawk still refuse, to this day, to peck in the dirt like a chicken. If he can't catch it on the wing, he don't bother.

That's it, the Tale is done. O
heaping pot of blessings, ibayo

BRER HAWK
& Sistah Sun

You may recall the year of the big drought, when everybody went hungry. One day Brer Hawk out in search of food when he happen upon Sistah Sun and mention his predicament.

Now, every once in awhile, Sistah Sun like a diversion from tending the earth all day. *I tell you what Brer Hawk*, she say, *Catch me before sunrise and I will turn the light down so Cousin Storm can bring some rain.*

Brer Hawk thank her profusely. But every morning when he rise, there Sistah Sun is doing her thing, bringing the heat. Brer Hawk get up earlier and earlier, but the Sun beat him every time. Then one morning, he hear Brer Rooster crowing a morning song, and he take it personal. *Don't mess with me, Brer Rooster*, he squawk. *Ain't in the mood for no mess.*

Brer Rooster ask him why he so quick to take offense where none is meant and Brer Hawk apologize, say Sistah Sun been ducking him, say he hungry and short-tempered. *Forgive me, Brer Rooster*, he say, but he looking at Brer Rooster all slantwise hungry and Brer Rooster step back on him. *How's the family*, say Brer Hawk, *They wouldn't, by chance, be out and about, would they?*

Look here, say Brer Rooster, *tell you what I'ma do. Sistah Sun pay me good money to wake her up every morning. Tomorrow morning, I'ma cry, Fly, Hawk, fly. That's when you catch up with her before she rise. Fly, Hawk, fly.*

Brer Hawk say he will stay over and rise up in the morning with Brer Rooster, just to be sure. Brer Rooster allow that might not be a good idea. *I'm a light sleeper*, he say, and *would not want you to stir about in your sleep and rouse me.*

But the Hawk insist he won't stir and the next morning find them out there, spying out the faint hint of morning, when Brer

Rooster begin to crow. *Fly, Hawk Fly. Fly, Hawk, fly.*

And Brer Hawk fly. Fly, Hawk, fly. With all his might he fly and he fly and he fly, till he come to Sistah Sun's house seconds before she rise. He push the doorbell and step back when she open the door, hair all mussed up and rubbing sleep from her eyes. *Morning, Sistah Sun,* say Brer Hawk.

What you doing at my door this time of morning, she say. He remind her of their deal and she look at him cross-eyed, *Common sense shoulda told you I didn't mean for you to come knocking on my door this early in the morning. Who gave you my address?*

Brer Rooster did, he tell her. *Well you can tell Brer Rooster to feed you,* she say, *because I surely won't.*

She slam the door on him and turn up the heat. Brer Hawk withdraw and fly back to earth. Brer Rooster still pecking in the dirt when Brer Hawk settle into the branches of a nearby tree. He still got that lean and hungry look about him, and Brer Rooster offer him a worm.

Worms don't suit a high flyer like me, say Brer Hawk, *that's for birds that don't fly.* Whereupon, Brer Hawk grab for Brer Rooster and Brer Rooster begin to crow: *Rise up, Sistah Sun, rise up. Rise up, Sistah Sun, rise up.*

Sistah Sun rise up so sudden she blind Brer Hawk with her light and in the confusion, Brer Rooster get away clean. Whilst Sistah Sun preparing for her day, she allow a deal is a deal and turn down the light so Cousin Storm come calling, and the drought is thereby broken.

Since then, Brer Hawk take on anything that hop, flop, fly or swim. Drought or not, he flexible. Long as he can take it on the wing, he flexible.

And every morning, without fail, Brer Rooster rise the sun. And all is right in the world. All things as they should be. All good. Ibayo. All good.

Rise up, Sistah Sun, rise up
Ibayo. Sistah Sun, ibayo

BRER RABBIT &
Brer He Lion

Very old stories, the best kind, will tell you not always the strongest nor the fastest, that's mostest in this world. More often it's the smartest that win. Brer Elephant strong, Brer Tiger swift, but Brer Rabbit has gotten the best of both.

So. Let me tell you how Brer Rabbit outfox King He Lion. This back when the King claim he baddest of the bad, so it is his right, he say, to be Kinging it over everybody else. Also, as King, he claim one offering per family, one lamb from the sheep, one kid from the goats, and so on like so.

Then come the time he sent word to the Rabbit Folk that it was their time to feed the King. Choose one of the Rabbit children and send them on.

Ms. Rabbit make it clear to her husband that will not work. *Might as well go yourself, if you think you gon send one of my children to feed that feline fool.*

So. It's face the King or Ms. Rabbit. Not even a contest. When he finally do approach the King, his fur is matted and his coat is in disarray, he limping and lame and bloodied up some. He has clearly been in a fight, and just as clearly lost it. *Morning King He Lion,* Brer Rabbit say all trembly. *I come to be the family offering.*

You look a little peaked there, Brer Rabbit, say King He Lion. *You sure you not sick? Hate to be put off my feed by some bad meat.*

I ain't at my best, Your Majesty, and my fleas have been monstrously busy at me, but I'd rather feed you than that beast I seen down by the river. He worse than you, Your Majesty.

Ain't nobody worse than me, Brer Rabbit. If that was so then they would be the King and not me. Just who is this fellow you referring to?

I was afraid to ask him his name, Your Majesty, he strike me terribly fierce.

What you mean fierce, roared King He Lion. *I will show you fierce,* he say. *Show me where this fellow stay.*

Don't want to do that King He Lion, say Brer Rabbit, *I'm afraid he might hurt you.*

King He Lion bristle UP on his hind legs and commence to roaring. *Afraid he might do what? Have you lost your mind? Lead me to him, Brer Rabbit. We will see who get hurt around here.*

So Brer Rabbit lead him down to the riverside, whereupon he tell the King, *That new fellow was right there in the water, Your Majesty, let me see if he still there.* Then Brer Rabbit look over into the river and jump back in alarm. *There he is, King He Lion, there he is.*

Tail switching in anger, King He Lion step up to the river and look over into the muddy surface of the water. There, staring back at him, he see another lion just as angry as he is.

He roar and he roar and he show his teeth. The fool in the water roaring just as loud, teeth just as long. King He Lion snarl at him, the fool snarl back. King He Lion so infuriated he leap into the river after him. But Mama Big Muddy run deep, she run strong, and just like that, she sweep King He Lion away. *Help me Brer Rabbit, help me,* he say.

Don't know about that, Brer He Lion, say Brer Rabbit. *If I save you, you will keep lording it over the rest of us, and eating up everybody's offerings.*

King He Lion say he won't do that no more. *Ain't doing no more hunting after this, Brer Rabbit, no more hunting, not a bit.*

Unlike Brer Wolf, the King of Everything known to value his word, and Brer Rabbit, for all his doing, aspire to be the better man. You will note perhaps that what King He Lion promising ain't what he was asked. But the Rabbit a softie at heart, a trait I myself find endearing. He pull King He Lion out of the river, and since then, King He Lion has kept his promise. Mostly.

King He Lion, he don't hunt nothing now, it's Queen She Lion do the hunting. King He Lion spend most of his time sleeping in the trees, cause he don't want to get caught up by that fellow snatched him into the river that time.

Better safe than sorry, he say.

I can't question that, likely God won't either, too busy Blessing multiverses, I imagine, ibayo

BRER RABBIT'S laughing place

One day before last, Brer Fox moseying down the road when he come upon Brer Rabbit laughing to himself. *What's so funny?* say Brer Fox. *You ain't laughing at me, are you?*

Naw, Brer Fox, I'm laughing cause I just come from my laughing place. Whilst I was there I stocked up on chuckles and got some to spare.

Brer Fox sigh and say, *Life been so hard on me I ain't laughed in most a week, Brer Rabbit. You think you can loan me some of those chuckles.*

I don't know, Brer Fox. As you well know, times is hard for everybody, and I need all the chuckles I can get. Never know when one gon come in handy. I tell you what I will do, though, I will take you to my laughing place, and you can pluck some yourself.

I appreciate that, Brer Rabbit, that's right neighborly of you.

So. Brer Rabbit take Brer Fox to a big clutch of bushes. *Here it is, Brer Fox. The laughing place.*

Brer Fox say he don't feel no more like laughing than he did a hour ago. He step up on Brer Rabbit with a big toothy grin and Brer Rabbit step back.

What you got to do, say Brer Rabbit, *is run up in there fast as you can, grab you some chuckles, and run right back out. Just as tickled as you can be.*

Brer Fox figure when he come running out, he will scoop Brer Rabbit up for supper. That will tickle him for sure. So he run up into the bushes and smack DA**B** into a hornet's nest.

Beset by angry hornets, he come out there faster than he went in. Brer Rabbit rolling on the ground, laughing fit to bust. *Ain't nothing funny that I can see,* say Brer Fox, *as he run briskly by.*

Brer Rabbit say, *I told you this my laughing place, Brer Fox, not yours. Not everything tickle me gon tickle you.*

Old Rabbit laughing all over himself. Problem is, whilst he laughing at Brer Fox those hornets take a notion to move him along, too. Fore you know it, him and Brer Fox running down the road together, just like the old friends they are.

**Walk in grace &
bless yo soul, ibayo**

BRER RABBIT &
Mama Big Muddy

In the Time before Time, Mama Big Muddy was clear as glass. She was a pretty young river then, water just as clear as a snowfed mountain stream. Back then she was known as Sweet Water River, and all the animals would come visiting, sitting by her banks fiddling, flirting, frolicking and frisking.

Then, one day on a notion, Brer Rabbit got to goading Cousin Rain and Cousin Wind about who the strongest. Told Cousin Rain that Cousin Wind was talking bad about her, told Cousin Wind the same. They decide on a race to see who the strongest of them all.

Back then, Sweet Water River was straight as a rail. Wasn't no river nowhere straight as Sweet Water. So on the appointed day and time, Cousin Wind and Cousin Rain lined up on her banks. Memphis to New Orleans. Let the best power win.

At the appointed hour, Sistah Sun step behind a cloud so as not to prejudice the proceedings, and when the shadow of those clouds fell on Mother Earth, it was on. Cousin Wind puffed herself up and commence to blow. She blow and she blow and she blow, stirring up dust all over the Delta.

But when Cousin Rain start pouring, all that dust turn into rich black mud, and when all that black mud start staining Sweet Water's skirts, she turn this way and that, trying to escape.

Finally, she got angry and she flood her banks, pouring rich black mud over everything in the neighborhood, feeding the

Delta and flooding folk out all the way down to the Gulf of Mexico.

Since then, folk back home call her Mama Big Muddy. Half water, half mud, all attitude.

Since then, she twist and she turn and she won't stay still. And every once in a while, she rise up and flood folk out, just to remind folk, in particular that silly rabbit, you don't want to mess with Mama Big Muddy.

Some folk claim its God's Will when Big Mama turn on them, but Big Mama don't pay them no mind. No more than Old Man Earthquake or Great Aunt Tsunami.

When the earth shift in search of its own equilibrium, folk suffer. When universes shift, planets die. Don't take it personal. There are songs far greater than any we sing. Ibayo.

May all the Gods be good to you
May the Gods be good to us all

BRER ROOSTER
free at last

Now, there some folk claim that what Brer Rooster saying in the morning is not, *Rise up Sistah Sun.* Some folk claim he singing, *Free at Last. Free at Last. Thank God Almighty, I'm free at last.*

What happened, these folk claim, is that one morning the Humanfolk was about to prepare Brer Rooster for supper. Had the long knife in hand when Sistah Sun to step out from behind a cloud and blind them so bad they drop Brer Rooster to the ground. I'm told Sistah Sun soft on Brer Rooster, I'm told she like his stylee strut. Whatever the case, next thing you know, she beaming all over God's heaven and the executioner drop Brer Rooster cold.

I'm free, yell Brer Rooster, *I'm free.* Then he make a break for it for the treeline, crowing, *Free at Last. Free at Last.*

CHORUS: THANK GOD ALMIGHTY, I'M FREE AT LAST

From that same treeline, Old Man Rabbit watching the commotion with acute fascination. *Peculiar, these Humans, just as peculiar as they can be. Should have brought the grandbabies,* he thinking. Little picninny don't believe when he tell them about the old days. About him and Fox, and Bear, about Big Mama Coon, Senator Terrapin, and them. He miss them all and wonder sometime, friends and enemies both, why he the only one left.

Why me, Lord, why me?

Old Man Rabbit stretch, working his shoulders, and using his

cane, he leverage himself upright whilst the galloping miseries settle where they please, and he think, with some regret, that all he good for these days is telling the tale.

Old Fox like to catch me so many times it ain't funny, he tell the grandbabies, when they sitting around in the fireplace evening, television off and the wireless down. Sharing you remember when stories.

Well, actually did catch me once or twice, actually, just couldn't hold me. Oh, I was handful in my day. Lions, Tigers and Bears, none of them could stand toe to toe with the Rabbit.

The kiddie rabbits squeal in rabbitish glee. Granrabbit telling lies again. *Ain't nobody slick as all that, Granrabbit. You so funny.*

Grandma Rabbit shoo them off to bed, and he fondly watch them go. Can't blame them for not believing. *Me and mine bout the only one left these days. Bear and Fox long gone, ain't that many Rabbits left. I hear Brer Coyote holding his own, and who knew Sistah and Brer Deer would flourish so, but when the last time you seen a Coon?*

These Humans not only peculiar, they dangerous, and when Brer Rooster drop from the Humanfolk hand, Rabbit motion him into the briar patch, quick quick.

Old boy Rooster run past the Rabbit without so much as a howdy. But every morning, some folk claim, in honor of the one that got away, you can hear Brer Rooster crowing—*Free at last, free at last.*

Thank God Almighty.
Free at last, Ibayo

BRER RABBIT
and the stars

L ast Brer Rabbit story I heard told was Brer Rabbit and the stars. I once heard any good story is at least 3 or 4 stories deep, and since this is a good story, I expect you to pay close attention to the weave of it.

First time the Rabbit went off planet, it was an accident. He had wandered in looking for some space rations, found himself a comfortable acceleration chamber and settled in for a quick nap. When he dream, he find himself in that awkward space between real and not real, the godhood, where every thought changes things, where next thing he know, they breaking free of the atmosphere and he is startled awake. After an initial panic, he decide to go along for the ride. Not that he had, at that point, much choice in the matter.

But when he found stowawaying, the crew determine they don't have the resources to carry dead weight. He will have to go out the shuttle port. Or maybe they should make a meal of him. Tasty rabbit stew be better than those space rations anyday.

Whilst they debating these matters, Brer Rabbit shut himself off in a command nodule and quick quick he hack it quick, drop the Conqueroo in the grid, and download the starmap program into his neurals. Then he erases Map everywhere, anywhere else, along with all the redundancies, whilst his neurals overload and his head e^{x}plo^d$_e$ with all the new knowledge. Knowledge that now only he know.

This cause much consternation. They didn't even know you could do that. His position now is he the only one know the way. *I am the master of this game,* he say, whereupon he demand to be made captain of the enterprise, or at least a valued crew member.

CHORUS: HE WHO KNOWS WHERE TO GO

Place assured, he look out on the great canvas of stars and see a universe of possibility.

Biggest briar patch he ever seen.

That is all. This Spell is done.
The Great Long Journey has begun
God's Blessings on us all, ibayo

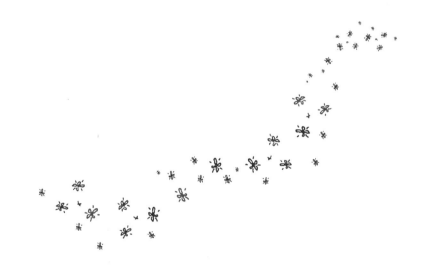

THE BRER RABBIT RETOLD PROJECT

The Brer Rabbit tales were originally oral stories told by slaves from the American South. After the civil war, they were gathered together in a written form by a journalist called Joel Chandler Harris. His frame story is that of an old slave – who appears to be a happy, contented slave – narrating these tales to a group of white children. So in spite of his sincere appreciation for the stories, critics have since pointed out a serious problem with his minstrelised version: Harris implies that slavery is a good thing. On the other hand, Harris can be seen as a man of his time, and the important thing is that he wrote the stories down. If he hadn't, these folktales might not have become the first body of African-American literature.

Based on this version, the tales began to travel and be re-told, largely as simple children's stories. But there was far more to them than that. "They're one of the tap roots of African-American literature and culture," says Arthur Flowers. He grew up on them, and had always wanted to re-write them. "For a long time I've wanted to take Brer Rabbit back," he says, "And do something that we could be proud of with the material. I wanted to revise them as wisdom tales."

Arthur's vision tied in perfectly with Tara's engagement with tradition – for more than two decades, we've been working on nudging traditional art and stories in contemporary directions, to come up with new forms without losing the essence of the original. So we asked him to feel free to experiment, and he not only came up with unique versions of the original stories but also added a few new ones – featuring Brer Rabbit, but also women characters who sometimes outsmart him. He also came up with a very distinctive narrative technique: a fusion of the western written and the African storytelling traditions.

In a sense, this entire project was about fusion and the making of connections.

DESIGN AND PRODUCTION

Book designers **Tanuja Ramani** and **Catriona Maciver** worked closely with our production team to realise the complicated steps needed to make this book. The book making artisans at Tara's handmade workshop created this book using two different methods of printing: the cover and the flat red layers of colour were silk-screened by hand, after which it was overprinted using a Risograph. The book was bound and numbered by hand, as part of a limited edition print run. This project is our latest effort at using local skills and resources to re-invent the art of fine bookmaking.

THE AUTHOR

Arthur Flowers, a Delta-based performance poet and writer, teaches at the English Department of Syracuse University in the United States. A native of Memphis and co-founder of The New Renaissance Guild, he considers himself heir to the western written tradition as well as the African oral one. He has written fiction as well as non-fiction, including *Another Good Loving Blues* and *Mojo Rising: Confessions of a 21ˢᵗ Century Conjureman*. *I See The Promised Land*, a life of Martin Luther King jr., was his first book with Tara. *Brer Rabbit Retold* is the second.

THE ARTIST

Jagdish Chitara is a folk artist from the nomadic Vaghari community, working in the Mata-Ni-Pachedi style of ritual textile painting from Gujarat, western India. He is based in Ahmedabad, and works in close collaboration with his family, who are also practising artists. He has participated in various government-run workshops and fairs within India. This is his third book with Tara, after *The Great Race* and *The Cloth of the Mother Goddess*. Watch a short film at tarabooks.com/mother-goddess-film to discover more about Jagdish Chitara and his exquisite tradition of textile art.

THE MUSICIANS

ARTHUR FLOWERS Vocals

SARATHY KORWAR Percussion

GANDHAAR AMIN Flute

VINAY KAUSHAL Guitar